# This Special Daddy Do My Hair book belongs to:

.......................................................................................................

.......................................................................................................

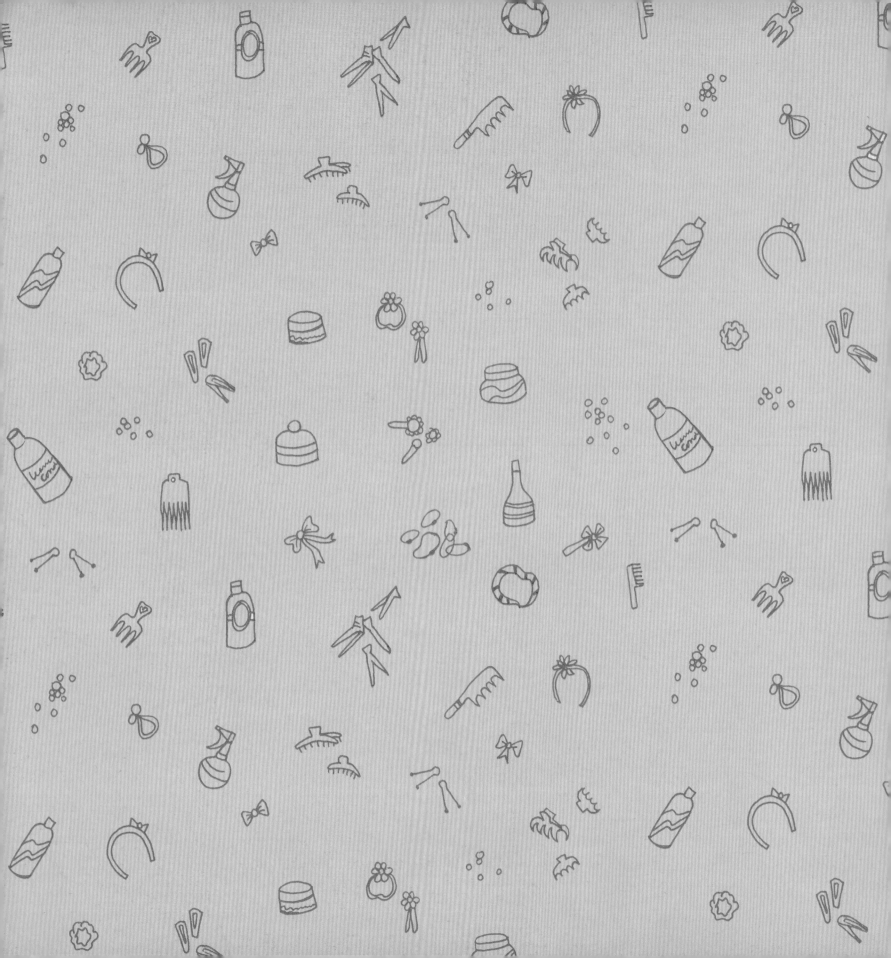

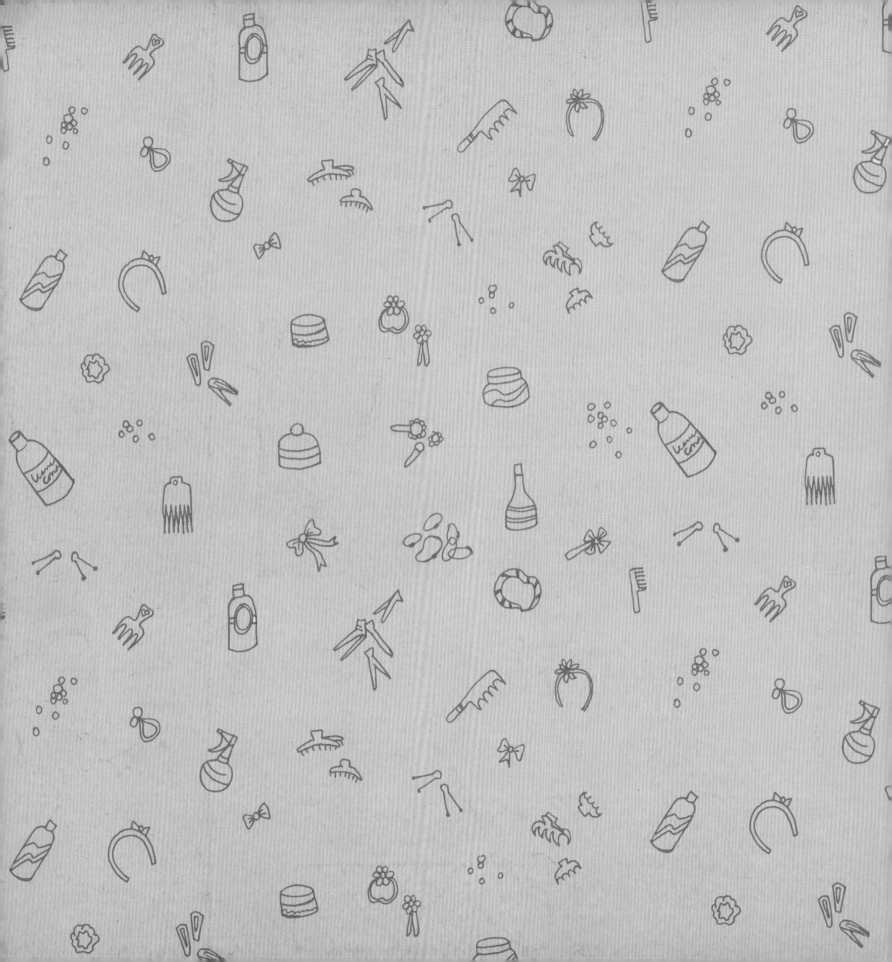

For Goziam and Elizabeth, the best daddy-daughter team in the world.

For my parents, thank you for believing in me.

First published in Great Britain in 2016 by Florence Elizabeth Publishing Limited
27 Old Gloucester Street, London WC1N 3AX

ISBN: 978-0- 9954869-0- 4
Printed in Turkey

\*

Books may be purchased in quantity and/or special sales by contacting the publisher,
Florence Elizabeth Publishing Limited
Tel: 0203 3847118
info@florenceelizabethpublishing.com
www.florenceelizabethpublishing.com

# Daddy Do My Hair?
## Beth's Twists

By Tola Okogwu

Illustrated by Rahima Begum

FLORENCE ELIZABETH PUBLISHING

It's Sunday evening and dinner is over.

Beth is excited and heads to the sofa.

Daddy is there with a smile and a chair,

"Daddy," she asks, "will you please do my hair?"

"Of course," says Daddy, and kisses her cheek,

For this is a question she asks every week.

This time that they spend is special and sweet,

Moments of fun that feel like a treat.

"How would you like me to style it today?

Bunches or pigtails, with a bow on display?"

"Can we do twists please? I'd like quite a few."

"A great idea Beth!

They'll look pretty on you."

He starts by parting her hair like a pro.

His hands are so gentle, they don't hurt her 'fro.

He twists the strands, but not too tight.

They hang down her back so bouncy and light.

They talk and giggle, tell stories, sing songs,

And have so much fun that it doesn't take long.

The next day at school, Beth walks in with pride.

Just look at her smiling, ever so wide.

Her friends are in awe and can't help but stare.

"My Daddy's amazing. He did my hair!"

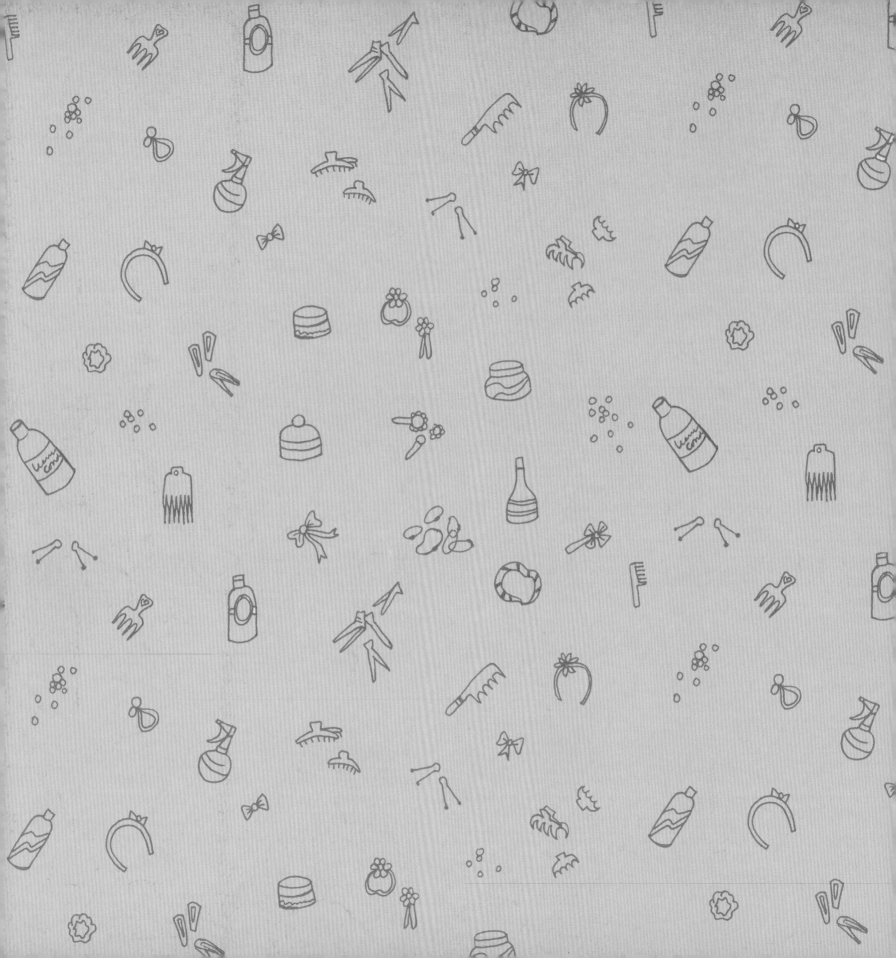

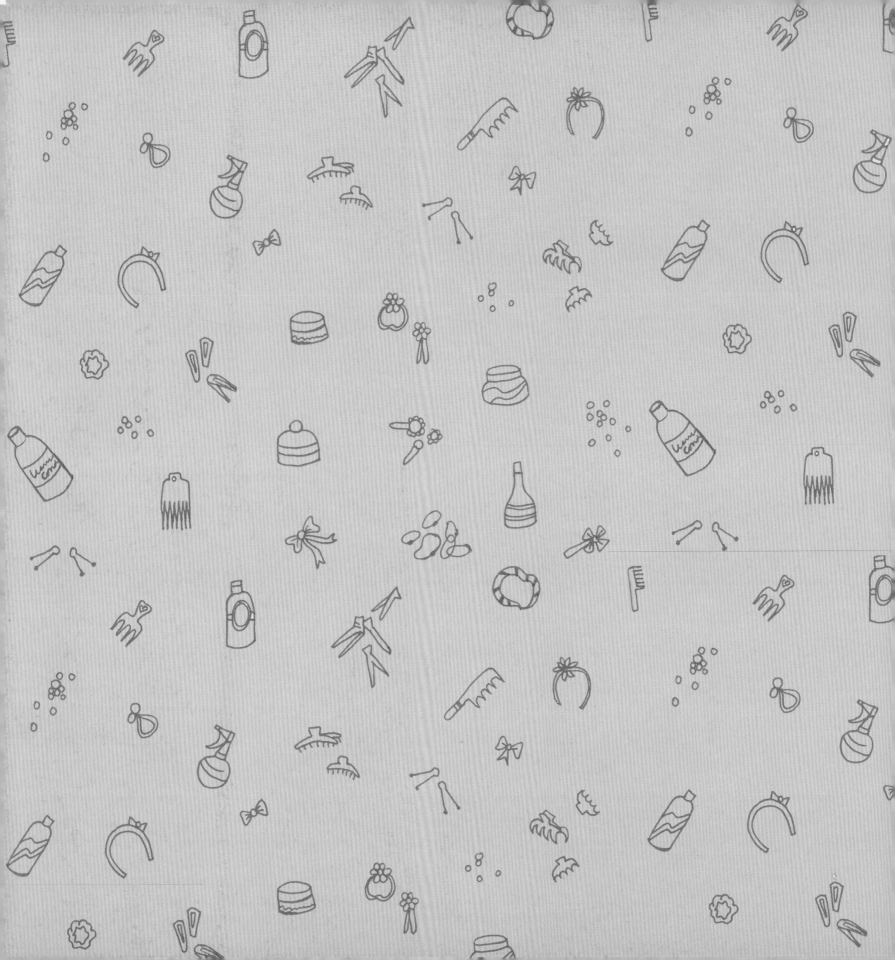

For more styles, resources and information
about the next book in the series go to

**www.daddydomyhair.com**

# More brilliant books
# from 'Daddy Do My Hair?'

978-0-9954869-2-8 (PB)

978-0-9954869-1-1 (PB)

For more information about the series go to
www.daddydomyhair.com